William Wild

by Lisa Thompson
illustrated by Wayne Bryant

Characters

Nina
Nina has freckles. She is crazy about horses.

William Wild
William likes catching lizards. His room is super messy.

Aunt Jen
Aunt Jen wears scarves on her head. She loves gardening.

Nina's mom
Mom has long, brown hair. She loves cats.

Setting

William's
Wild
Kingdom

Contents

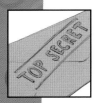

Chapter 1

The Night Stranger

Nina was putting her cat, Frankie, outside when she saw a black car glide to a stop across the road. Out stepped a boy with three, large bags. He wore a top hat and a long coat.

"It looks like Jen's nephew is here," said Nina's mom. "He's staying with Jen for a week. His name is William."

Nina was excited to have someone
new to play with on her street.

"What's he like?" asked Nina.

"Jen calls him William Wild. She says he's *very* wild. You'll find out what he's like tomorrow," smiled Nina's mom. "Jen's invited you over to meet him."

9

Nina realized that she didn't know much about William's Aunt Jen. She lived across the street at number 7 Maple Lane. She liked gardening, and she sometimes waved hello, but that was all.

With a name like William Wild, thought Nina, he can't be boring.

She was right. Boring was one thing William Wild was not.

Chapter 2

Captain Wild

The next morning, Nina opened the front gate of 7 Maple Lane. Someone shoved a long piece of bamboo into her hand.

"Shhhhhh!" said William Wild. "Protect yourself. A band of space pirates from the planet Ziro 245 has entered our galaxy."

"They are in search of galactic treasure!" said William Wild. He was dressed from head to toe as a space pirate.

"Galactic treasure?" asked Nina. "William, where are we?"

"I am Captain Wild, fiercest pirate in 27 galaxies. It's lucky you arrived when you did. What's your name?"

"Nina," said Nina in a whisper.

"First Mate Nina," said Captain Wild,
"put on this helmet. You'll need it!"
William gave Nina a plastic bucket.

"You are now a crew member of my intergalactic spaceship. Come and help me protect my treasure."

Captain Wild pulled the cover off of
Aunt Jen's giant wheelbarrow.

"Gardening tools!" laughed Nina.
"This is your treasure?"

"These aren't gardening tools," said Captain Wild. "They are precious treasure! They are simply disguised so the space pirates won't be able to find them."

"Hurry," said Captain Wild. "The space pirates have just landed. We must hide the treasure!"

Captain Wild and First Mate Nina grabbed all of the treasure they could carry. They dragged it into a large hole in the middle of the back garden. Then they covered it.

William ran to the spigot and turned on the hose. He filled a bucket with water and detergent. Bubbles foamed up and over the edge. The froth flowed along a sheet of plastic.

"Beware of the alien slime!" cried the
Captain. "It eats away at your skin."

The backyard was suddenly full of
alien slime. They both ran and slid
for their lives.

When it was time for Nina to go home, she was a very happy, space pirate covered in alien slime.

Before Nina left, William's Aunt Jen asked her, "Have you seen my gardening tools? I asked William, and he said he doesn't know what I am talking about. He said aliens must have taken them."

Chapter 3

The Wild Ninja

The next day, Nina walked through Jen's gate and up the front path. She thought, I wonder where William . . .

Suddenly, William jumped out from
behind a plant.

"Halt," he said. He blocked her way.
"It is I, the Wild Ninja. I cannot let you
go inside. There is a scary dragon on the
loose."

"Dragon?" giggled Nina.

"Yes," said the Wild Ninja. "The Emperor has told me that I must catch it. Are you brave enough to fight the scary dragon?"

"Of course," said Nina.

"Here is a special fire sword. It is for fighting dragons. Follow me." William handed her a long, green stick with a strange, bird-like flower at the top.

The dragon lived down the side of the house. The ground was slippery with dragon goo. It smelled like rotting plants. Garbage cans, buckets, and tools blocked their way.

A gardening fork was jammed between two cans.

"Behold, the Wild Dragon!" said the Wild Ninja. He grabbed the gardening fork. The Wild Ninja stabbed the fork into the side of the dragon bag.

The dragon's smelly guts poured out onto the ground. Nina climbed onto the back of the dragon. She took out its teeth. The dragon roared and shook. The Wild Ninja fought it to the ground.

"Our kingdom is saved!" cried Nina.

The Wild Ninja asked Nina to kneel
so that she could be knighted.

"Arise, Dragon Ninja!" he said.

When it was time to go home, Nina felt as brave as a real ninja.

William's Aunt Jen told Nina to come back and play the next day.

She also asked her if she knew where her gardening fork was.

"William says he doesn't know what I am talking about," sighed Aunt Jen. "He says a dragon may have eaten it."

Chapter 4

The Wild Wicked Wizard

The next morning, Nina made it into the gate, up the path, and almost to the front steps of the house before she found William.

This time, William was dressed as a fierce wizard. Her cat, Frankie, was by his side.

"We've been expecting you," he said. "I am the Wild Wicked Wizard. I've been sent here to make a powerful potion. As my helper, it is your job to find the following things for the job. Do not fail me!"

The Wild Wicked Wizard let out a horrible cackle. He then handed Nina the list.

1 Spider's web
4 snail shells
3 leaves
6 flowers
3 eggs
5 scoops of slug filled dirt
3 liters of water
1 apple core

Nina collected all the things on the list.

The Wild Wicked Wizard poured all the ingredients into Aunt Jen's giant gardening bucket. It was a gooey mess with a nasty stink.

The Wild Wicked Wizard and Nina stirred the potion. They poured it into smaller containers. They made a huge mess.

Nina couldn't believe the day was over already. It had gone in a flash. It was time to go home!

William invited Nina back to play the next day.

His aunt asked Nina if she knew where her big, gardening bucket was.

"William says he doesn't know what I am talking about," Aunt Jen said, shaking her head. "He says maybe it just disappeared in a flash!"

Chapter 5

Inspector Wild

The next day, Nina walked through the gate of 7 Maple Lane. She walked up the path and climbed the steps to the house. She had never managed to get this far before.

Nina waited on the top step for William.
But he did not come. Finally, she knocked
on the door. Aunt Jen opened the door.

"Hello Nina," said Aunt Jen. "You're looking for William? I'm sorry. His mom came and picked him up last night."

Nina's head dropped with disappointment.

"You don't know where my gardening gloves are, do you?" asked Aunt Jen.

Nina shook her head.

"William said he didn't know what I was talking about. He said maybe they were hiding," she sighed. "He did leave this for you, though."

William's aunt handed Nina a large
envelope. It was stamped **TOP SECRET**.

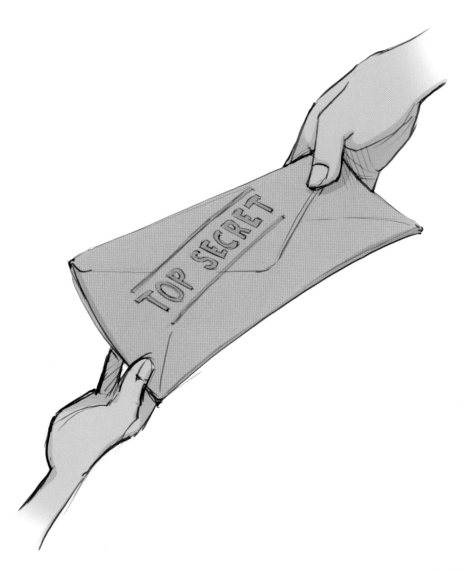

Dear Inspector Nina,

My sources tell me that a pair of top-secret, spy gloves are hidden in my aunt's garden. Your mission, if you choose to accept it, is to find the gloves. They will lead you to three growing rubies. You have half an hour to finish this task.

Signed,
Inspector Wild

William's Aunt Jen also read the letter.

"Well, we'd better get to it," she smiled.

Nina and Aunt Jen split up. Aunt Jen looked in the garden shed and found the stinky potion in her gardening bucket.

Nina looked around the back garden. All she found were bits of dragon. Aunt Jen met up with Nina in the front garden. There was no sign of spy gloves.

Time was running out.

Then, Jen saw something on top of the tomato sticks, in the vegetable patch.

"I see them!" she cried, racing across the garden.

She put the gloves on and crouched down low. It was time to look for the growing rubies.

A twinkle of light flashed from a tomato
bush. Nina leaned in to take a closer
look. She saw another flash of bright
light.

Three large, red tomatoes had tiny, shiny gems stuck to their skins. They glittered in the sunshine like rubies. Nina picked all three, just in time.

"Mission complete!" she cried, handing the tomatoes to Aunt Jen.

Aunt Jen held up her beautiful, ripe tomatoes.

"William really does have a *wild* imagination," she sighed.

Glossary

cackle
a noisy, witch-like laugh

detergent
liquid used for cleaning and washing

disguised
made to look like something else

galactic
something from the galaxy

ingredients
parts of a mixture

knighted

to be awarded for outstanding actions; to be made a knight

mission

a special job for someone to do

ninja

a Japanese fighter

potion

a poisonous or magical drink

Looking at a Narrative

Introduction
(Who? What? Where?)

Who?
Nina
William Wild
Aunt Jen

What?
Nina sees that Aunt Jen's nephew has arrived. His aunt calls him William Wild and Nina is looking forward to meeting him.

Where?
In the garden at Aunt Jen's house

Problem
(What happens? What goes wrong? How does the character feel?)

PROBLEM 1

Nina goes to play with William. William asks Nina to help him defend the garden from alien space pirates and a dragon.

PROBLEM 2

Nina and William hide the treasure from the alien space pirates and save the kingdom from the scary dragon. Wicked Wizard William needs Nina's help to find the ingredients to make a powerful potion.

PROBLEM 3

Nina successfully finds all of the ingredients for the potion. The next day Nina is disappointed to discover that William has gone home with his mom. But he left her a top-secret mission she must accomplish.

Resolution

(How the problem is solved)

Nina and Aunt Jen accomplish the mission. They find the spy gloves and the three growing rubies.

Adjectives to look out for

precious	*wild*	*scary*	*special*	*bird-like*
smelly	*powerful*	*gooey*	*stinky*	*ripe*

Connecting words to look out for

Suddenly	*The next morning*	*Before*
The next day	*This time*	*Then*

Author Lisa Thompson

Who is your hero?
The bright spark who invented fire starters. They make camping a lot easier!

What is the best advice you have ever been given?
One of my favorites is, "See it, believe it, achieve it."

What is your favorite place to go on vacation?
Besides somewhere where I can ski, it's a little secret beach down the coast.

How long is your little finger?
Long enough to reach the keys on the keyboard. Phew!

What do you like to do on your birthday?
Talk to the Queen and thank her for her generous gifts!

Illustrator Wayne Bryant

Who is your hero?
Master Yoda—not because he is a wise and powerful alien, but because he is cute, and he talks funny.

What is the best advice you have ever been given?
Always say please and thank you.

Where is your favorite place to go on vacation?
Breamlea Beach. It's a beautiful surf beach that nobody else knows about, so don't tell anyone, OK?

How long is your little finger?
It's exactly the same length as my nose.

What do you like to do on your birthday?
Fly to Breamlea in my own helicopter, but I don't have a helicopter yet.